Jacques Chessex is one of Switzerland's greatest
living writers. He is revered in France and won the
Prix Goncourt in 1973 for *L'ogre*. His other works
include *Monsieur* (2001), *L'économie du ciel* (2003)
and *Pardon mère* (2008).

# THE VAMPIRE OF

# ROPRAZ

## Jacques Chessex

Translated from the French
by W. Donald Wilson

**BITTER LEMON PRESS**
**LONDON**

BITTER LEMON PRESS

First published in the United Kingdom in 2008 by
Bitter Lemon Press, 37 Arundel Gardens, London W11 2LW

www.bitterlemonpress.com

First published in French as *Le vampire de Ropraz* by
Bernard Grasset, Paris in 2007

Bitter Lemon Press gratefully acknowledges the financial assistance
of Pro Helvetia, the Arts Council of Switzerland

swiss arts council
prohelvetia

This book is supported by the French Ministry of Foreign Affairs as
part of the Burgess programme run by the Cultural Department of
the French Embassy in London (www.frenchbooknews.com)

© Éditions Grasset & Fasquelle, 2007
English translation © W. Donald Wilson, 2008

A CIP record for this book is available from the British Library

ISBN 978–1–904738–33-6

Typeset by Alma Books Ltd
Printed and bound in the United Kingdom by
CPI Cox & Wyman, Reading, Berkshire

# The Vampire of Ropraz

A little dead girl says:
I am the one convulsed with horror
in the live woman's lungs.
Get me out of here straight away.
    Antonin Artaud, *Suppôts et supplications*.


Ineligible are: citizens excluded for reasons
of mental illness or feeble-mindedness.
                    PUBLIC NOTICE,
            Municipality of Ropraz,
                12th January 2006

# Preface

When I came to live in Ropraz in May 1978, Rosa Gilliéron's grave still lay intact along the path in the graveyard that's on the way to my house. It was a slab of sandstone surmounted by a small pillar of white marble wreathed with roses of tarnished brass, bearing the name and dates of the deceased. The top of the little column was broken off to show the brevity of a life cut short before its time, turned to tragedy, in its bloom of perfect promise.

Rosa's grave was abandoned ten years ago, when the graveyard was renovated.

# 1

Ropraz, in the Haut-Jorat, canton of Vaud, Switzerland, 1903. A land of wolves and neglect in the early twentieth century, poorly served by public transport, two hours from Lausanne, perched on a high hillside above the road to Berne, bordered by dense forests of fir. Dwellings often scattered over wastelands hemmed in by dark trees, cramped villages with squat houses. Ideas have no currency, tradition is a dead weight, and modern hygiene is unknown. Avarice, cruelty, superstition – we are not far from the border with Fribourg, where witchcraft is rampant. They hang themselves a lot in the farms of the Haut-Jorat. In the barn. From the ridge-beam.

A loaded weapon is kept in the stable or cellar. With hunting or poaching as a justification, they cherish powder, shot, great traps with metal teeth, and blades sharpened on the whetstone. Fear lurks. At night prayers of conjuration or exorcism are said. They are severely Protestant, but cross themselves when monsters loom in the fog. Along with the snow, the wolf returns. It is not so long since the last one was killed, in 1881; its stuffed hide is gathering dust seven miles away, behind glass in the Vieux-Moudon museum. And then the fearsome bear that came from the Jura. It disembowelled some heifers not forty years ago, in the gorges of the Mérine. The old folk remember it; there's no joking in Ropraz or Ussières. In Voltaire's day, when he lived in the château down in the hamlet of Ussières, brigands would "wait" on the main road – the one leading to Berne and the German lands – and, later, soldiers returning from Napoleon's wars would hold honest folk to ransom. You have to take care when employing a vagabond for the harvest, or to dig potatoes. He is the outsider, the snoop, the

12

thief. A ring in his ear, a crafty look, a knife in his boot.

Here there are no large shops, factories or plants; people have only what they win from the soil – in other words nothing. It is no kind of life. People are so poor that our cattle are sold to city butchers for meat. We make do with pig, and so much of it is consumed in every shape and form – smoked, rind removed, minced or salted – that we end up looking like it, with pink faces and ruddy jowls, far from the world, in dark coombs and woods.

In this remote countryside a young girl is a lodestar for lunacy. For incest and brooding in unwed gloom on flesh for ever desired and for ever forbidden.

Sexual privation, as it will come to be called, is added to skulking fear and evil fancies. In solitude, by night, the amorous romps of a few fortunate individuals and their moaning accomplices, satanic titillations, a guilt entwined into four centuries of imposed Calvinism. Endlessly construing the threat from deep within and from without, from the forest, from the cracking of the roof, from the wailing of the wind, from the beyond, from above, from beneath, from below: the threat from elsewhere. You bar yourself inside your skull, your sleep, your heart, your senses; you bolt yourself inside your farmhouse, gun at the ready, with a haunted, hungry soul. Winter stirs this violence beneath the lasting snow, a friend to the demented, the ruddy and bistre skies between daybreak and night-time deprivation, the cold and the gloom that strains and wastes the nerves. But I was forgetting the astounding beauty of the place. And the full moon. And the nights when the moon is full, the prayers and rituals, the bacon rind rubbed on warts and wounds, the black potions against pregnancy, the rituals with crudely fashioned wooden dolls stuck with pins and martyrized, the spells cast by charlatans, the prayers to cure spots on the eye. Even today in sheds and attics you still find books of magic and recipes for brews of menstrual blood, vomit, toad spittle and powdered viper.

*When the moon shines too bright, beware bric, beware brac. When the moon rises rathe, shut up serpent in sack.* Hysteria swells. And fear. Who slipped into the loft? Who walked on the roof? *Look to pitchfork and powder, before secrets of the abyss!*

# 2

February 1903. The year started out very cold; the snow is lying on Ropraz, which seems more huddled down and neglected than ever on its wind-beaten plateau. Since the first of February the snow has been falling without end. A heavy, damp snow against the dark sky, and for some time the village has had no relief. Blocked roads, fevers, several cows miscarried, and on the seventeenth, which fell on a Tuesday, young Rosa, a big fresh flower, twenty years old, clear skin, big eyes and long chestnut hair, died of meningitis on the farm of her father, M. Emile Gilliéron, Justice of the Peace, and member of the Grand Council. He is a man of some stature, severe, sensible and generous. He is wealthy, owns quite a lot of land hereabouts, and his daughter's supple beauty had aroused powerful emotions. She also sang well, was devoted to the sick and was an active parishioner in the mother church in Mézières… Folk out of the ordinary, as you can see. Surprisingly, given the ugliness, vice and meanness all around…

The news of Rosa's death moved the whole countryside terribly. They came to the funeral, in the Ropraz graveyard on Thursday the 19th of February, from distant villages, towns, hamlets and far-off ridges. By cart, on horseback and on snow-shoes they came, men and women in such numbers – several hundred – that despite the cold the chapel doors were left open throughout the entire service, and the procession from chapel to graveyard took over an hour, to the constant tolling of the death-knell.

To make room for his newest lodger, Cosandey the sexton had to dig down into the frozen earth. Job done. In the middle of Thursday afternoon, Rosa Gilliéron was buried on the south-east slope, two thirds of the way down the graveyard, which stretches, solitary, between the thickest of the forest and a wide, deserted hilly area over which crows fly, cawing. Once the coffin was closed and the last handful of frozen soil had dully thudded down on its wooden lid, there was no need for Cosandey to spread snow back over the little plot. After the interlude that had allowed the procession to follow the hearse, just as the final prayer was being said, and the children had sung for the last time, and Pastor Béranger, come specially from Mézières, had given the blessing, the snow began to fall again, the snow that cloaks the black earth of old winter and gently lulls the dead – we are assured – in their eternal rest.

After his daughter's burial, Gilliéron had arranged for refreshments in the Grande Salle. That is the name given to the hall where festivities and official events are held. Then evening brought parting handshakes and embraces; the roads and unpaved tracks were deserted, and a long night descended on the desolate landscape.

Friday the 20th; snow and immobility. One would almost have thought that Rosa's death and the prolonged ritual in the graveyard had dulled spirits and stunned the countryside into stupefied silence.

# 3

But now it is Saturday the 21st. This morning
very early at first light, François Rod, who lives
above Ropraz in a locality called Vers-chez-les-
Rod, has decided to "go wooding" in the hilly
forest that borders the graveyard lower down.
His son Hermann is with him, leading the heavy
ox-cart used by dairy farmers and woodcutters.
It is half-past seven. The sun is rising slowly over
the snow-covered countryside. The lane to Tailles
Wood runs beside the graveyard. Coming to the
gate in the railings, François stops the team, tells
his son to wait for him, and makes his way into
the graveyard, intending to say a prayer over
Rosa's fresh grave. He takes a few steps down the

path and immediately cries out: Rosa's grave lies open, her coffin laid bare. Seventy years later the aged Hermann still remembers his father's cry, "as if he'd seen the devil himself" he would say, trembling, his eyes shot with red, still raw from fear even at this great length of time.

On the cart, Hermann is petrified; François comes staggering through the gate, not even stopping to close it behind him, falls in the snow, gets up, falls again and finally stumbles along to the Auberge Cavin. Cavin appears, old Mme Cavin and Cosandey the sexton.

They return to the graveyard. The light is full by now, a sickening white. Around the open grave are footprints – the ground is quite trodden down – and the outline of a body stretched out, a storm lantern half-buried in the snow a few metres away. Cosandey climbs down into the grave. The coffin lid has been completely unscrewed and hastily replaced, leaving a narrow gap near the dead girl's chest. Cosandey puts his hand through.

"I can't feel her head!" he howls, collapsing, doubled up over the coffin.

Cosandey is revived and, shivering, remains behind to keep guard by the grave; the others make for the Cavin café to use the only phone in the village. Those expected are M. Gloor, Justice of the Peace in the Mézières district, M. Blanchod, the examining magistrate and two officers of the canton's *Sûreté*. It will take them three hours to reach the Jorat by the wheezy old tram that runs between Lausanne and Meudon. To make up for lost time they will be fetched by cart from the halt for the château at Ussières.

Then come the discoveries. From Mézières, where they finally managed to reach him, Dr Delay has come to join the group. He orders the coffin lid to be removed. The body violated. Traces of sperm and saliva on the victim's naked thighs. And the bloodiest mutilation is revealed in all its horror.

The left hand, cleanly severed, is lying beside the body.

The chest, hacked with a knife, has been entirely butchered. The breasts have been cut off, eaten, chewed and spat into the sliced-open belly.

The head, three-quarters detached from the torso, has been pushed down into it after bites were made in it in several very visible places: the neck, the cheeks, the base of the ears.

One leg – the right one – has been hacked up the thigh to the genital cleft.

The pubic area has been sliced away and chewed, devoured; what remains of it, some pubic hair and cartilage, will be found where it was spat into what is called the "Crochet hedge", two hundred metres above the forge.

The intestines are hanging out of the coffin. The heart is nowhere to be found.

It is clear that the madman removed the body from the grave to handle it with greater freedom. A fistful of long hair and two large pools of blood, partly soaked up by the snow, lie near the desecrated grave.

The horrible work done, the bestial meal consumed, the young martyr's body was put back into the coffin, in its place in the wide-open grave.

# 4

The Vampire of Ropraz. The expression was born two days later in the *Feuille d'Avis de Lausanne*, when the newspaper wrote in its issue of 23rd February:

This sorry affair will no doubt have painful repercussions in our district. Never before have the annals of crime been obliged to record such an abominable act in Switzerland. It is highly desirable, for the public's peace of mind, that the guilty party be apprehended by the justice system and receive the exemplary sentence he so richly deserves. Hyenas have hunger as an excuse for disinterring the dead. For this

25

individual, this despicable *vampire*, we can find none.

The Vampire of Ropraz, the rapist, the bloodsucker of Tailles Wood, the bat of country graveyards... All Dracula's team is abroad, galloping through the land. At the same time the case is spread by the press all over Europe and America, and newspapers from New York, Massachusetts, Boston, and of course from England and Scotland, the land of gothic fantasy, are delivered to the municipal clerk's office in this village, the grisly fame of whose graveyard spreads shame and terror all around. It is strange to open these great dailies from so far away, and find huge headlines printed over four columns of frightful details: "VAMPIRE OF ROPRAZ".

It does not take long for the investigation to bog down and become sidetracked. It first makes for Vucherens, a nearby village, to interview the Caillet brothers, some rather sinister individuals with previous involvement in murder, extortion, theft and banditry. Six years earlier, at Écoteaux, old man Caillet, his eldest son and the mother had murdered Budry, a dairyman. The father and son were sentenced to life and the mother to three years as an accessory. The father and mother had died early in their prison term. But the *Feuille d'Avis de Lausanne* recalled in its issue for 23rd February that, by a most curious coincidence, Rosa Gilliéron was the daughter of M. Émile Gilliéron, who had presided over the jury called upon to pass sentence for the Écoteaux crime.

Vengeance, then? A crazy vendetta by the two younger brothers, thirsting for blood? But the Vampire had acted alone. The two Caillets are depraved and violent, but not mentally deficient. Still, they had recently bought from the Mézières general store some shuttered lamps of the same type as the one found at Ropraz. And they are virtuosos with the knife. Where were they on the night of Thursday the 20th to the morning of the 21st? They are arrested, but then released. Their womenfolk, also the lowest of the low and equally fit for the gallows, provide them with alibis.

In the meantime, rumours grow. And so does the fear. People arm themselves more than ever; at night they bar themselves in, and denunciations are rife. Envy, base jealousy, pretenders rejected by Rosa or her stern father, individuals injured by the judge's decisions, political hacks with noses out of joint at his success, solitary, timid individuals, the desperate and the compulsive, obsessed by the purity of the all too lovely girl... Another name is bandied about: that of a prominent inhabitant of Ropraz, whose second profession as an itinerant butcher working from farm to farm could suggest obscene, iniquitous uses of the knife. A cutter-up of pigs and sides of veal! He becomes the target of the most scurrilous insinuations. For an entire week suspicion falls on a medical student who had come, just at the end of February, to spend a few days with his family in Mézières. A budding surgeon, just think, with all those anatomy classes taught at our expense!

The student is grilled for two entire days on the premises of the *Sûreté*. A sheer waste of time.

"A tough nut, that one," says Inspector Decosterd, who is leading the investigation. "Not easy to intimidate, these young doctors. Anyway, we're keeping an eye on him. He says he's going to be a surgeon. All the more reason not to lose sight of him for a single second..."

In the meantime, the Vampire is on the loose. He is reported in Vucherens, Ferlens and Montpreveyres, always appearing at night, evading the watch and the dogs, climbing on each occasion to the upper floor, where the daughter of the house or the maid sleeps.

"Look at the broken pane, that's where he rested the ladder..."

"But he didn't harm your daughter."

"She woke up in time. She was dreaming, poor thing, and suddenly she started to scream. We barely had time to grab an axe and run upstairs."

People are frightened, stupefied, curious.

"He didn't touch her, the bastard, but he was there all the same, just look at the broken pane, and there, where the snow melted on the wood

29

floor. You have to think he was scared off by the cloves of garlic and the crucifix she was sleeping with!"

For everywhere folk have again taken out the Christ they've kept hidden since Catholic days. Now, in every village and hamlet, you can see braided garlic and the holy images repugnant to the monster of Ropraz hanging from the window frames and catches, from lintels, balconies, railings, even from secret doorways and in cellars. Crosses are erected again in this Protestant countryside where none have been seen for four centuries. On hills, beside country roads, the object abominated since Reformation days is erected again. The vampire fears the symbol of Christ? "There, that'll make him think twice! And the dog is loose."

Pastor Béranger and the mother parish of Mézières tolerate these superstitions. "With the Fribourg witches and their priests and deacons so near, right on the border, I'm used to that kind of nonsense." Bérenger is a Huguenot. A soldier of Christ. As Rosa's religious instructor, he was present when the body was pieced together again, after it was brought back from the graveyard to the Grande Salle for a few hours to be washed and repaired. It was he, Bérenger, who blessed the remains, which were dressed once again in a fresh white gown before being reburied.

"But what about Mme Bérenger, and the little girl that helps in the manse, aren't you afraid the monster will go after them, Pastor? He must want to avenge himself on you, you who were so kind to Rosa…"

"The man who loves God need not fear the spirit of darkness," replies the pastor steadfastly.

And he climbs back onto the seat of the horse-drawn cart that he drives himself. Night is falling, a haunted night; for a long time his wheels can be heard crunching through the icy snow on the road lower down.

# 5

In the meantime he is up and abroad, the Vampire of Ropraz, a distant cousin, and so like him, of Drakul, master by moonlight of the crime-ravaged steeps of Walachia and Transylvania. The fearful resemblance of the Carpathians and the Vaudois foothills is in his favour, with their dark forests where he can hide and keep watch, sharpening his hunger and thirst, the one who devoured the pure Rosa.

Make no mistake about it, crouching in the bushes where he will lie low till the sun goes down, or in a hillside cave, in the crevice of some dark cliff, he heard the pastor's cart as it rattled along the stony track. Later he is sure to have seen the lamps extinguished in the windows of the château of Ussières, the lamps put out in the Cavin café, in the solid stone dwellings, in solitary farmhouses. Now the night belongs to him.

The wind has risen from the coomb. It chills the night, a damp, cold wind that keeps dogs in their kennels and hardens the ice on country roads... So many young virgins are sleeping their lily-sleep in so many dizzyingly warm beds. So many dead girls will spend their first night in the soil, beneath the covers of their fresh graves. It is time to be about, Dracula, master of the shadows, through town and country! You who know our every gesture, our stopping places, our hesitations, who will drink our daughters' blood, ravish them, consume them, before dawn pushes you back into your inaccessible lair!

For since 20th February you would think there was no hill, no wood, no side road safe from the monster's power. He is everywhere, the Vampire of Ropraz, prowling, watching, lurking; because of him fear swells, ingrained in solitary farms.

The dread of a shocking discovery haunting the more substantial properties, the obsession with sexual, expiatory violation engrafted in the flesh. The ancient guilt of bodies punished, offered to the Devil.

You were too lovely, Rosa, you must pay for your blinding purity!

For generations all has been perilous and evil in these lonely landscapes: the storm that swells the rivers, the lightning that sets roofs on fire, the drought that kills crops, bakes grass, shrinks and shrivels fruit, the rain that rots the harvest and furrows the ploughed field. People distrust tramps, beggars and itinerant preachers, all as light-fingered as gypsies. Travelling people, Bohemians, Romanies. Pedlars are driven off at pitchfork point. But now it is 20th February, now is the reign of the Vampire, the embodiment of every fear, violence and repressed hysteria, the compression into something intangible of the dreaded secrets of an evil world. Pastors denounce our pride and lies. Sunday sermons in Calvin's churches remind us of the judgement in store for our heedlessness. There is, above all, welling up from generations of tortured brooding, the assurance of punishment from on high suspended over our lives.

Now, in the Vampire's grip, no hovel, great dwelling or tiny house, no shed, hut or bothy, can escape his cruel vigilance. The children from lonely houses no longer go to school, the postman no longer makes his daily round in hills or hamlets, and Dr Delay is protected by the game warden when he travels to see a distant patient. But have people even the right to fall sick in such dire times?

More than ever, mothers watch over their daughters. Before February the danger was boys, dances, lotteries, sing-songs, but now the monster is concealed among us, cunning, clever, all-knowing, about to lick his lips and drool over our slumbers before puncturing the throats and smooth bellies of our fiancées.

On Monday the 2nd of March, 1903, an indignant editorial appears in the *Revue de Lausanne*: "THE VAMPIRE OF ROPRAZ STILL ON LOOSE".

The reactionary newspaper has blazoned across four columns:

It is unacceptable, all the same, that our police, normally so expeditious, are still unable to find any clue that would enable them to confront the odious criminal who is sowing terror throughout our countryside, soon to turn his attention to our towns and public occasions. Will the abominable violation of the remains of young Rosa Gilliéron, whose eminent father is the judge and councillor Émile Gilliéron of Ropraz, remain unpunished for much longer? Is the Vampire thumbing his nose at public order and the peace of an entire countryside, of which he will soon be master?

These lines, like the articles now appearing in newspapers all over Switzerland, and more and more frequently in Europe, perfectly express the disquiet and impatience agitating public opinion and incensing town and country. On the one hand, the Vampire, thumbing his nose at everyone, doing as he pleases, and making the hysteria mount. On the other, the impotence and inaction of the investigation. One gloomy question punctuating the article in the *Revue de Lausanne* sums it all up: "When can we expect the next infernal episode?"

# 6

March went by, and then April: veiled insinuations, false reports, an uneasy calm; nothing more has happened since the outrage in Ropraz. But rumours swell, names are bandied about, lawsuits for libel and slander are threatened. Factional disputes, family hatreds, obscure quarrels over wills or property boundaries: so much baseness that springs to life out of fear and suspicion.

In cutting up and sucking the corpse of Gilliéron's dead daughter, the Vampire of Ropraz has set the judge's followers at each other's throats. At the beginning of March, one of his neighbours from La Moille du Perey, a prominent local personality and rich landowner, was rumoured to have made

Rosa pregnant. All the judge's authority and Dr Delay's testimony would be needed to silence a calumny that no one believed. Rosa had died pure from all suspicion, but the ugliness of the attack showed what malevolence was in the air.

Around the same time, a bachelor from Hermanches, Juste Fiaux Esquire, blind in one eye and a born loser, was arrested by the *Sûreté*. Throughout the summer of 1901, this Juste Fiaux had worked as a labourer on the Gilliéron farm, incessantly pestering young Rosa with his inappropriate advances, as is duly attested. She gently rebuffed him, and that was the end of it. But could the embittered Fiaux have avenged himself for the slight? This lead was soon dropped.

And what of that portly peripatetic butcher in Ropraz, whose name has been mentioned as an enemy of the council representative? He engaged a lawyer from Lausanne, Maître Spiro, a fearsome cross-examiner, and no one hereabouts wanted to be subjected to one of his celebrated onslaughts. Exit the peripatetic butcher, cattle dealer, large farmer, and parish councillor by occupation.

Others were less fortunate. The name came up of a schoolmaster who had been dismissed for an accusation of molestation that was never completely resolved; the fellow's name was never cleared, even though the teacher took up new work as a public letter writer in Oron-la-Ville. There he wrote (or had written) the strangest kind of love letters – to ladies of Oron and Mézières, to young women all over the district, to Dr Delay's daughter, to Rosa. The writer denied everything. Where was he from the night of the 20th to the morning of the 21st of February? He claimed to be unable to say, in order to protect a lady's honour.

"And the day before?"

"I was working on my novel."

"Did anyone see you at your desk?"

"I don't make a spectacle of myself. Do you know what it means to write? A sacrifice. Yes, gentlemen, a much more terrible sacrifice than that of some innocent country girl's remains!"

Inspector Décosterd and his colleagues in the *Sûreté* tapped their foreheads with their index fingers. A writer! And a modern martyr too! The oddball was left to his ranting.

So things remain until school opens again after Easter, on Tuesday the 14th of April. The outrage takes place at Carrouge, almost five miles from Ropraz, where the road to Moudon goes uphill. In the area between the graveyard and the school that serves as a playground, the schoolmaster Aimé Jeunet, who teaches in Carrouge's one-room school, smoking a little Fivaz cigar while he supervises playtime, has his attention drawn to a group of children enjoying a game of football with a strange ball. Going over to them quietly, Aimé Jeunet discovers to his stupefaction that the ball is a head, and that the head has lost its scalp and is covered in blood, with tufts of hair still adhering to the skull like some repulsive adornment. The teacher almost faints from horror, and the boys scatter. For Jeunet has recognized the head: "It's Nadine!" he cries, staggering again and falling flat in the grass.

Over the next hour the grim ritual is rediscovered in all its horror. The open grave, the coffin lid unscrewed and, once again, the corpse violated, with traces of sperm and saliva around the navel and on the thighs. And the rest of the body defiled and bloodied: this time the girl's genital area has been removed, her head entirely severed from the trunk. Then the head was scalped, as can be seen from the cuts in the bone, the encrusted blood and the long tuft of black hair that lies gleaming on the sunlit path.

What had happened at Carrouge?

Three years earlier a village family had taken in an orphan who had survived tuberculosis of the bone. But one leg remained crippled, and Nadine Jordan had a limp. She was given light housework to do to earn her keep. She was pretty, conscientious and fresh-faced; the boys began to court her despite her stiff leg and her still childish figure. She was well proportioned, with an attractive bust and long shining black hair: the schoolmaster himself, M. Jeunet, was not indifferent to her charms... But a hard winter gives no quarter. The preceding December her tuberculosis became active again, a nasty fever gained the upper hand, and death soon followed: Nadine Jordan died a few days before Easter, on Thursday the 9th of April. She would be buried on Saturday the 11th. As in Rosa Gilliéron's case it was Pastor Bérenger – Carrouge is not far from Mézières – who officiated at the burial, speaking of Nadine's brief existence as a courageous, spotless young girl, and reciting the prayer for the dead.

This time there was no snow to preserve the Vampire's tracks. There was this severed skull covered in black blood, and a long handful of hair, still pearled with red, lying in the grass of the graveyard, behind the church and the school.

# 7

Spring seems to arouse the Vampire's ardour. Scarcely have Nadine Jordan's tortured body and scalp been discovered at Carrouge, when the Jorat is again stunned by a third macabre affair.

This time it happens at Ferlens, a village to the east of Carrouge, on the road to Lake Bret. A young woman of twenty-three has just died of tuberculosis, and her husband, Jacques Beaupierre, has granted her last wish to be buried with her head resting on the little rubber cushion that helped her endure her suffering. A strange wish, and a promise piously kept: Justine Beaupierre is buried on Tuesday the 21st of March, her head resting, inside her coffin, on the absurd but serviceable object.

Imagine Beaupierre's horror, on his first visit to the graveyard, when he sees the aforesaid cushion, orange-coloured and very easy to spot in the nine o'clock light, on the path leading to his wife's grave!

Once again, an open grave, a gaping coffin, a burial gown torn away, the young woman's throat pierced and slashed, her breasts sliced off and partly eaten. Dried sperm and traces of saliva like animal slaver, as Jacques Beaupierre would later describe it, around the navel and in the creases of the groin. The belly is sliced open with a long, neat cut; the pubic area and genitalia have been excised and removed. Pieces of them, chewed and spat out, hair, tender flesh and cartilage, will be found in the boxwood coppice that runs along the graveyard fence. Just as scraps of the pubic area and hair were found in the dark Crochet hedge in Ropraz, after the February outrage.

"The colour of Justine Beaupierre's eyes?"

"Brown, darkish in shade."

"Colour of her hair?"

"Dark brown."

"The complexion of the aforesaid?"

"Pale and clear."

"The height of the aforesaid?"

"Medium, well formed. Well-developed breasts. Narrow hips."

"Build of the aforesaid?"

"Slender and willowy. Ninety pounds at most."

You would think that the Vampire of Ropraz keeps to one type of woman, always the same, and that he selects his sacrificial victim well in advance. Where does he get his information? How does he know that a dark, slim girl is dying, and in what precise location? Does he have a list of the young patients near death in all the clinics, sanatoria, isolation wards and nursing homes in the country? Has he an accomplice in the Moudon hospital? And the times of the funerals: how does he know the very day, the very hour, that such and such a young woman is to be laid to rest in such and such a village?

People begin to suspect churchwardens and undertakers, and the one in Ferlens, old Cordey, is grilled by the investigators. Thanks be to God, he is saved by the bottle. At the time of the Beaupierre crime, Jérémie Cordey was still dead drunk, thanks to the tips he had been given the previous day.

Justine Beaupierre is reburied. Once again a new gown for the massacred corpse, and once again Pastor Béranger, not fearing to compare these dreadful events with the Ten Plagues of Egypt, with the merited punishment of Sodom and Gomorrah. "What crime are we paying for, miserable creatures that we are? Thou knowest, O Lord, and we know too, if only we look deep into our hearts. None is innocent before the Lord. It is only after we have examined all our sins, and decided to repent, to change the direction of our lives, that Thou, O Lord, wilt restore peace to our towns and villages. As Thou hast, in Thy goodness, bestowed peace upon our hearts benighted by so much error."

There, it has been said: God will destroy the Vampire once we have surrendered to Him. A biblical vow, commensurate with the obsession with sin engrafted in the bodies of Calvinists in their wasteland. Their souls in despair at the steep ascent to a heaven that is out of reach. Béranger knows his people well. However, especially after night has fallen, everyone thinks of the three lovely bodies, bloody and cut to pieces deep in their fresh beds of soil in the three lonely little graveyards, and they know that the monster will have the last word in this vale of bitter tears and richly deserved darkness that God has granted us.

# 8

The Beaupierre crime in the Ferlens graveyard, in its rehearsal of the ritual, had surpassed the worst imaginings. Would there ever be an end to this butchery?

A new incident at Ferlens, the "Café du Nord affair", as it was instantly baptized, might have given the impression that the guilty party had been caught.

The owner of the Café du Nord, M. Georges Pasche, had been complaining since winter that in the cowshed adjoining his farm and café – which together formed a single, sizeable building – his cows and heifers were being subjected to unnatural practices. Indeed, that winter, and all through the spring, the vulvas, anuses and recta of several animals had been injured by the introduction of a penis of large proportions, a stick or pick handle, or some other pointed instrument, for the membranes and recta of the young females were found to be punctured or torn, very often bleeding, at morning milking time, and the orifices of several animals were still smeared with sperm.

At first Georges Pasche kept watch, not daring to reveal what was happening for fear people would accuse him of dealings with the Vampire of Ropraz. But as it continued, and even grew worse, Pasche finally offered two five-franc pieces – heavy silver coins of the Federation and a substantial sum in this countryside at the time – to whoever would denounce the guilty party or help to surprise him. It is Monday the 11th of May, 1903.

Nothing more was needed, just two days after the reward was announced, for the little serving girl from the café to catch Favez, the farmhand, in the cowshed in the middle of the night, standing on a stool with his trousers around his ankles, busily having his way with a hobbled heifer. The little serving girl held up the lantern: "This time I've got you, my lad!" Pasche comes running when he hears the fray, and old Madame Pasche, and of course the Pasche children, all in their nightshirts in the cowshed, which reeks and fumes with heavy smells, steam and brandished oil lamps. The labourer is forcibly dressed, tied up and shut in the cellar, to wait for the police from Mézières to lift him into their van at dawn, and lock him up in the prison in Oron, the chief town of the district.

The full name of the unfortunate fellow is Charles-Augustin Favez. He is twenty-one years old, but looks twice that: strangely deformed, receding brow, alcoholic, perverted, taciturn. And he pleasures himself on our animals! Maybe he haunts graveyards too? What if Favez were the guilty one, Favez at Rosa's grave, Favez at Carrouge, Favez at Ferlens too! Of course it is Favez, sadist that he is. Favez is the monster. He is the Vampire of Ropraz. With no human victim, he perforates cows and heifers as he waits for other dead young women to come his way.

Or maybe living ones, who knows? Warm little quails in their innocent slumbers, schoolgirls, girls in catechism class or young mothers for him to lie on top of and rub his foul snout against.

On that Thursday, the 14th of May, a single cry goes up from the Jorat and from farther abroad across the whole countryside: "They've caught the Vampire! He's the Vampire!" Yes, that's him all right, worse than the legendary wolf or bear, the one who desecrated the bodies of three young dead women in Ropraz, Carrouge and Ferlens, the one who spread terror among us, and who now will be judged, the one for whom the ultimate punishment must be brought back. That morning, in the countryside and villages, everyone is talking about the death penalty, even though it was abolished thirty-six years ago.[1] Only the death penalty is appropriate, in the firmly held opinion of the entire population, for such abominable offences.

---

1. The last execution in the canton of Vaud took place at Moudon, about seven miles from Ropraz, on 15th November, 1867. The poisoner Héli Freymond, murderer of his own wife among others, was beheaded in the public square before a perfectly contented crowd.

But who is he, this lover of dead girls, this abuser of cattle and author of so many terrible crimes?

Charles-Augustin Favez was born in Syens, a tiny village between Moudon and Mézières, on the 2nd of November 1882, in a deprived environment in which drink, incest and illiteracy were family scourges. At the age of three Charles-Augustin was taken from his wretched family and given to a couple who abused him, before being finally placed by the welfare services in a family of shopkeepers in Mézières, who tried to give him a decent upbringing by having him do odd jobs around the shop, while at the same time he was attending school.

Charles-Augustin was a very sturdy lad, physically developed beyond his age and subject to dreadful fits of anger. He spent little time with his schoolmates, avoided girls and spoke so little that you might have thought he was dumb. Making his annual health examination in the Mézières schools in June 1892, when Charles-Augustin was ten, Dr Delay noted in his report that the Favez boy was over-developed for his age, extremely pale, with raw, red-rimmed eyes seeming "as if the daylight causes him pain". This remark would be cited in court.

Charles-Augustin Favez is subject to "absences" that obliterate from his memory certain facts or actions to which he has been subjected or that he may have committed. He seems to have cultivated these absences as a defence against serious hurt done to him in childhood, such as the hunger and ill treatment to which he was subjected before being placed with the Chappuis. In the matters of interest to us, he says he had no recollection of any of the recent perverse acts he has committed, or may have committed, in any of the graveyards mentioned.

It is discovered that ever since he was fifteen he has had a liking for drink that makes him imbibe whatever strong stuff he can get his hands on, especially on Saturdays, when he was seen in cafés and at dances, even when he was still under age, or at travelling fairs and other festivities, where he got drunk. On many occasions he has been picked up after closing time and dumped at the door of the Chappuis' shop on the Grand Rue, where people find such a spectacle alarming.

At sixteen he was expelled from catechism class for stealing fifty centimes from a fellow pupil's smock in the presbytery vestry. An interesting coincidence: at school and in catechism class one of his fellow pupils was Rosa Gilliéron, from whom, intimidated, he kept his distance, though the master's report says that "he watched her continuously and followed her in the street, even when her father was present".

There was just one year's difference between Charles-Augustin Favez and Rosa Gilliéron, born in 1882 and 1883 respectively. They had the "same" schooling in a district where public education was obligatory for all. It is strange to imagine the pure young girl innocently following the teacher's lesson from the front row, while from the back of the class Favez the Vampire is watching her and already imagining he is drawing her blood and feeding on her.

# 9

So Favez is locked up in Oron prison. He is not held for long: only fifty-seven days. How is it possible for the most notorious criminal in all Switzerland to escape punishment in this way?

In Oron, contrary to every expectation, Charles-Augustin Favez will benefit from the interventions of two individuals. The first is inevitable: it is by a psychiatrist already famous at the time. Dr Albert Mahaim, a student of the theories of Charcot, who had attended his lectures at the Salpêtrière Hospital in Paris, has himself carried out a considerable amount of research on hysteria, sadism and neurasthenia, and senses in Favez an excellent subject for observation, and possibly for corroboration, useful to the development of his own theories. A professor in the Lausanne Medical Faculty, Albert Mahaim is also one of the founders of the Cery psychiatric institution, to the west of the town, on the wooded fringe of the community of Prilly-Chasseur. The ambition of the Cery institution is to grow into one of the most important European centres for the study of mental illness. For instance, shortly after it opened in 1873, thirty years before the events related here, the institution established several geriatric wings and a model farm, where the less dangerous patients, or those who, in the terminology of the time, were in a "latent" phase, were allowed to work, to the extent that they demonstrated their ability to do so. There were orchards, a market garden, forestry, poultry, tillage and livestock too – the Cery herd, with several prize-winning bulls each year at the canton's agricultural fairs, was soon considered one of the best cared for in the region. Already in 1903, the farm employed forty or so residential patients under the supervision of several doctors and overseers.

Albert Mahaim examines Favez and finds him to be an alcoholic, taciturn, inclined by his atavism to fits of anger that are liable to escalate into violence. But perhaps Favez is not the monster that people think. In any case, not a dismemberer of corpses or a cannibal.

His physical examination of Favez finds that he has a very robust physique and an uncommon tolerance of hardship. A tree that fell in the forest, during an unfortunate time of his life when the subject was working under a master woodcutter, has injured one of his shoulders seriously enough to leave him with a slight dislocation between bone and collarbone. But it causes Favez no pain, his upper body is powerful, his arms long and very muscular, his penis and testicles very well developed. A notable detail: as a consequence of frequent masturbation from an early age, the foreskin has been pulled back from the glans; the solitary practices of the subject have circumcised him naturally.

"Has the subject had sexual relations with a woman?"

"Despite his reticence and after many hours of talking, the subject admitted that he has never been with a woman. He has had encounters with prostitutes in Lausanne and Yverdon, but had had too much to drink and the women did not insist."

"The subject has a strong constitution. Why has he not done military service?"

"The army rejected him because of his disjointed shoulder. It is the right shoulder, used for shooting. The army physicians who examined him concluded it was a congenital malformation making him unfit for service. Too bad for the federal army," adds Dr Mahaim with a smile, "he would have made a good soldier."

However, one detail puts Dr Mahaim on the qui vive: Favez's eyes are always red and inflamed as if ringed by raw flesh; he blinks continuously, as if the daylight causes him pain. Albert Mahaim notes this detail with reluctance, knowing that he is endowing Favez with the red eyes of a vampire, unable to tolerate the light of day.

His injured, lopsided shoulder will always make his gait look as if he is fleeing, another characteristic of the monster.

A further detail, and one that takes on its full meaning if we remember the particularly long, sharp teeth of the nocturnal prowler with his thirst for blood: Favez's dental examination finds a jaw with abnormally long teeth, incisors sharper than is natural, which force his mouth open in a rictus that is difficult to look at.

As for the search of the personal effects of the accused, of his clothing and of the attic where he slept in Mézières, under the roof of the Chappuis' shop, it reveals nothing of interest, apart from a little wooden-handled pocket knife with a dull, rusted blade. A pathetic object, as Dr Mahaim demonstrates and explains, unable to cut into flesh with the quick and terribly effective precision of the three graveyard assaults.

The pocket knife is examined by two forensic experts brought in especially from Basle and Zürich, Dr Paulus Betschacht and Professor Johannes Berg, two experts consulted by the police forces of both Germany and Austria in murder and vice cases. These two austere gentlemen find no trace of human blood on the unremarkable blade, merely some fatty residues with a casein base, and fructose left by the cheese and the apples stolen from orchards that frequently provide the subject's only nourishment.

"So there was no blood, or trace of human fat in the accused's clothing either? Or on his footwear? In his bed?"

"No physical trace. The subject himself is clean, and the attic where he sleeps regularly is well aired and swept out by himself."

Also worth mentioning is that the Swiss-German experts, criminological specialists with European reputations, tested Favez on several pieces of animal flesh, ordering him to slice and cut up a beef carcass, a pig's belly and the breast of a young cow. The defendant showed that he was incapable of doing so. Whether using his "little knife" or with the help of extremely sharp butcher's utensils, Favez could not, or did not know how to, slice the meat of an animal slaughtered the evening before.

Dr Mahaim's concluding recommendation was that Favez should be released as soon as possible. A release accompanied by a fine of thirty-five francs for unnatural practices towards animals, and entered in the penal record, together with psychological supervision for at least three months, with an order to attend at the Cery institution on the first day of each week. Dr Mahaim added that at Cery he personally would see this Charles Favez, since in the course of his brief investigation he had become attached to an individual who was more a victim of rural poverty than the tormentor of a society unwilling to allow him a chance in life.

# 10

What a vampire dreams at night, bolted with three padlocks within his medieval jail – he reimmerses himself in scenes of childhood where he is dying of hunger, suffering, enduring, submitting and so often wishing for death. Locked in his cell in Oron's gloomy prison, Favez relives very old scenes he thought he had been able to wipe from his memory when he was free to roam. As a hunter, an avenger thirsting for blood? He is three or four, it is before the welfare services place him in Mézières, with the Chappuis; he is with his parents, the blows rain down, there is shouting, his father yelling and his fits of drunkenness, and the hunger, and the beatings, always the beatings and the hunger.

There is the miserable nourishment stolen from the children he rarely dares approach. There are the leftovers of rotting meat and old bones stolen from the dishes of the neighbourhood dogs. And later, after a long-drawn-out period, always the same in its sadness, a new family for him – he is four, maybe five – people he does not know and of whom he immediately feels afraid. It is in a remote hamlet among hills and ravines, beyond Vucherens; the man takes him on his knees and makes him lower his trousers so that he can put his big thing into him. Be quiet, Favez, no one can hear you. We're all alone here, just me and you, Charles Favez, little poor boy, there's only me and you, and you are going to let me have your little hole the way you did yesterday evening, and this morning too. Turn around Favez. Suck, Favez. Cry, Favez. And be quiet. Anyway, what happens here will never get out, never, there's just me and you, Favez, and my wife, the big sow, who will join in the dance. The man cries out, I wipe myself with my fingers, the palm of my hand, the sticky stuff is drying on me, and it hurts, I've bled again. Then the whip. Or the belt, the stick used for driving the swine. The man beats away, I am on my knees, my buttocks are bare, the man keeps hitting me and puts his big thing in my hole again.

And his wife? In the fields, his wife. In the forest to fetch firewood. The man is an invalid. A bad leg. Never leaves the house. Stays shut up with me. Once when I was on the ground, with his big thing well in, his wife suddenly appeared in the room, and right away got undressed and came to rub her hairy underbelly, her moist slit, all over my head and mouth. Stinking slit. And oozing. She cried out and kept rubbing away and crying out, and I still had his big thing in my hole and it hurt.

Later I was with the Chappuis and I was able to sleep in peace. No more big thing to hurt me. But the big thing's woman, his wife, that one, if ever I get my hands on her…

Who among your torturers do you ever find again? Violent male rapists with women looking on, saying nothing, vicious, who allow the child to become a prey, or use him for their own ends. In his cell Favez wakens in a sweat, drinks from the water bucket, and goes back to sleep under his coarse sheet. It is a sleep haunted by the figures, of women especially, who, now that the child is at last a man, will have to be made to pay, to pay for their cruelty with an even greater cruelty. One without witnesses. Without limits. And that day will come, you are sure of it, child now almost a man. You can't wait, Charles Favez? It will be that night. Or all those nights in the dark cold, or warm darkness, in the snow, at night or in the spring, to make someone pay for that filthy slit.

Cannibalism, offences against three dead young women, bestiality, aggravated rape: Dr Mahaim's sense of the source of the "mania" is of no help to him. As he thoughtfully explains, he feels doubt, loses all assurance, knowing only that he is far from imagining the specific martyrdom suffered by the child Favez before his placement in Mézières. All those years of crucifixion from abuse, from the sperm, the mucous of wanton brutes. "People talk about the 'Vampire of Ropraz'," notes

Mahaim in the register of his observations. "It is a popular, terrified simplification for the rapist, the necrophile, the dreaded consumer of the dead. In this wilderness, the vampire will live on as a symptom of evil, live on for as long as this society remains a victim of primordial squalor: the filth of bodies, the promiscuity, isolation, alcoholism, incest and superstition that infest this countryside and will create other sources of sexual exaction and merciless horror."

# 11

The second individual's involvement is still a mystery. On one of the first days of Favez's imprisonment, on Saturday the 16th of May, at six in the evening, a mysterious lady dressed in white gets out of a horse-drawn carriage at the gate of Oron prison. A coachman in dark livery waits for her on his seat. The gate is opened to let the lady in, and she enters the building; on Saturdays there is only one warder, who escorts the mysterious woman to Favez's cell.

He opens the door and leaves; the lady goes into the cell, closing the door behind her with the key given to her by the warder when she came in.

Favez is not expecting this visit. He is standing, tense, his features showing the bewildered suspicion of a prisoner ready to defend himself against a blow, against ill treatment. The woman draws nearer, looks him up and down from head to foot, and then gazes directly into his face. So this is he, the woman-eater. She draws even closer. The one who drinks young women. Favez can smell his visitor's perfume. She breathes in the smell of jailbird, the smell of death-lover. She draws even closer. Favez pulls back. Suddenly the woman extends an arm, clasps Favez, pressing herself to him in an almost convulsive embrace; Favez falls; a prolonged shudder runs through the woman, thrusting her against the prisoner. It is unclear what happens next. After half an hour the warder glues his ear to the cell door; later he will talk of a moaning, or groaning, or whimpering, he doesn't know which; it was "like a beast being strangled".

Who is this mysterious woman? There will be decent talk of a pious woman come to bring divine succour to a social outcast. Others, more pedestrian, but failing to solve the mystery of the strange intruder, will speak of a prison visitor – a novel career at the time – but, more realistically, others surmise that she is an adventuress thirsting for potent emotions, or even a fashionable sufferer from hysteria with the ability to pass herself off as a do-gooder in order to get close to a man who embodies her fantasy. A fantasy of sucking or ghoulish gorging. Of unnatural practices. One thing is sure: she paid the warder to allow her access to the Vampire. Several months later, when Favez was sentenced to the heaviest penalty available at the time, life imprisonment, the warder, called upon to explain himself and subjected to a strenuous interrogation by the *Sûreté*, would admit to having accepted several sums of money in coin and fifty-franc notes.

For the woman would return. During the two months of Favez's incarceration, she would seek him out on at least three occasions, as the warder's secret accounts testified. When the white lady, the mysterious woman, shuts herself in for over an hour with the man of graves and perforated heifers, the warder is riveted to the door; he is shaking too, the warder, he is dizzy at the moans coming from the shadows over and over, and at length, in the prison, where he is alone with the frantic couple.

Even today no one knows who the lady in white was, or who gave her away. For two centuries the Oron prison has been housed in a wing of the château above the town, its access making it difficult to watch from outside. The château stands on rather a high outcrop that discourages observers from either town or country. The lady in white must have been well acquainted with the locality and usages of the district. Nevertheless, she took a risk in gaining entry to an official building to seduce an individual accused of extremely serious crimes.

Was the white lady a doctor, as some supposed at the time? Maybe she became acquainted with Favez's case at the Cery clinic, from Dr Mahaim himself, or by stumbling on his papers. Could she have been a medical student, or some idle, wealthy auditor of Dr Mahaim's lectures, excited to the point of distraction by the person of Favez and his crimes, always sexual in nature. Hysteria, as is well known, draws in the deranged, as do seminars analysing the ecstatically possessed.

The warder was suspended. But having shown remorse, and being responsible for children in the town of Oron, he was restored to his position on condition he turned over his revenues to the abstinence society recently founded in the canton, bearing the empyrean name of "The Blue Cross".

# 12

Favez is set free on Thursday the 9th of July. His release from prison provokes outrage. The Vampire of Ropraz is free! In vain the justice authorities defend themselves, citing the psychiatrist's report, the expert witnesses from Basle and Zürich, the complete lack of proof regarding the three graveyard crimes and, above all, the decisive factor in the eyes of justice, the manifest inability of Favez to cut up or dissect any kind of flesh – animal flesh during the tests to which he had been subjected, or human flesh in the worst of cases. A vast, angry murmur sweeps through the countryside, and there are fears for the safety of the wrongly accused, considered a vampire by the public, fears of a lynching or a kidnapping followed by extreme abuse. Everywhere in the overwrought countryside, groups of "rural youth" are formed, with banners, posters and noisy meetings at which Favez's name is called out and chanted: "DEATH-TO-FA-VEZ, DEATH-TO-THE-VAM-PIRE", to the point that the police in Oron receive an order from the State Council, Justice and Police Service, to protect the outcast and repress the public disorder. But Favez has vanished. Fled, the Vampire. Gone. Without a trace. Where can he be hiding on these July days, when the popular rage is calling for his head? Later, people will imagine that the mysterious woman in white sheltered him in some hideaway where she could vampirize the Vampire as she pleased. Has he gone to earth in the foothills of La Broye, or maybe in the gorges of the Mérine, behind gloomy Villars-Mendraz, living on roots, river water and whatever he can forage from isolated farms? During this period people point to the theft of chickens from farmyards, of rabbits, of cheese set out in the open to dry on wooden racks. Gypsies? Tramps? Or Favez in his solitude, hunted, starving, making do with what he can find in the wild?

The unfortunate Charles-Augustin will commit the irreparable.

Is it because he has tasted the flesh of the white lady in his cell in the château of Oron? It seems that masturbation can no longer satisfy him. In his hideout Favez is almost dizzy remembering the advances of the Dubois woman, a flirtatious widow of Mézières, who had often titillated him with various provocations. The widow Dubois is fifty years old, dark and buxom, with a gleam in her eye, and moistens her lips with her tongue when she meets young men, bats her eyelids and laughs very loudly. Her bedroom window overlooks the Chappuis' shop; from his attic on the upper floor, Favez has often spied and studied her. He has met her in the town, and once she even dragged him into her stairway, laughing and wriggling, but Favez took fright and ran off. Among his bushes, along his side roads, he thinks of the widow Dubois, again sees her proffered bosom, her white neck, her firm thighs beneath the housecoat.

Favez has come closer to Mézières. On Wednesday the 15th of July, prowling around the outskirts, he stole a chest of spirits from the tram depot and drank all day, ten pints of abominable "schnapps", a mixture of apple and pear, leftovers from nobler, more sought-after distillations. He slept off his liquor in the thickets around Carrouge, dozed a little, and spent the rest of the night prowling around the widow's house. At dawn he saw her open the shutters, push open the window, and lean on the sill in her nightdress. She has seen him. He is sure of it. He returns to the tram depot, breaks open a case of spirits, and steals another bottle, which he polishes off without taking a breath.

It is 8:45 in the morning of Thursday the 16th of July, 1903. Intoxicated, slowed down by his effort not to stagger and collapse, Favez walks along the single street of Mézières and enters the passageway of widow Dubois's house. One flight, two flights; he knocks on the door, the

82

widow opens. It is later revealed that he threw her violently down on the bed, tore off her nightgown, bit her on the mouth and neck until he drew blood – as the red marks attest, real holes that remain visible for several days – then spread her legs and quickly entered her, in spite of the blows she was raining on him. The widow screams, the window is open, two customers from the Chappuis' shop rush in, followed by the widow's grandson, the young Justin Dubois, aged fourteen, on a visit to his grandmother that morning.

Favez, wild-eyed, his member still erect, is overpowered and his clothes are put on.

An hour later he is in the hands of the police, who again lock him up.

At noon that day a great crowd assembles in front of the Oron police station – in the same building, on the first floor, are the offices of the judge of the District Court, the Justice of the Peace, and a branch of the *Sûreté*. There is rioting, threats, angry chanting: "DEATH-TO-THE-VAM-PIRE, DEATH-TO-THE-VAM-PIRE," chants the crowd, moving off towards the château, where the accursed creature is under lock and key. Several policemen on horseback will be needed to block the way of the most incensed, especially those from Ropraz, who want Charles-Augustin Favez dead to avenge Rosa Gilliéron – the first victim of the Vampire drunk on blood and human flesh – and rid the countryside of the monster poisoning its existence.

# 13

In his cell, Favez is frightened. At any moment the triple-bolted door may give way under the weight of the rioters. Favez knows that the people of Ropraz are especially vindictive. He has been about long enough to know the tenacity of these country people. He knows he is *their* Vampire. One of the ringleaders would only have to decide – Aloïs Rod, Pierre Gilliéron or big Desmeules, who knocked out three fairground men by himself at the last Marksmen's Festival – for the barrier of police to give way and his cell door to shatter. Charles-Augustin Favez has often wandered around Ropraz; he remembers the girls' beauty, especially Rosa's; he gazed at her so much in school and later at dances and sing-songs that his eyes still hurt. The hills of Ropraz. The pink château. The other château, on the hill. And the graveyard before the forest, the Ropraz graveyard with its secret passage leading into the woods and gorges.

Favez is frightened. This evening, Thursday 16th July, it must be warm and bright outside; men and boys from Ropraz have come back to shout in front of the prison, and it is always the same cry that Favez catches, the chant that puts a knot in his stomach:

DEATH-TO-THE-VAM-PIRE
DEATH-TO-THE-VAM-PIRE

In his cell Favez is frightened. Why has the warder not brought him his soup yet? Why can he no longer hear the police detachment's horses in front of the jail? That is what is happening all right. That evening the police have returned to their station, leaving the field open for the men and boys from Ropraz. They will smash down his door, those men as hard as nails, they will beat him with a cudgel, break his bones and teeth, and then drag him out into the courtyard to drive a spike through his heart and burn him alive. Or they will bring him back to Ropraz, a stake will be set up by the chapel, and he will be roasted, he, Favez, naked and screaming as the whole village looks on, avenged at last.

Favez goes over to his bed, places his hand on the rough sheet. Linen, the sheet. Strong. Mechanically, the prisoner begins to tear away the hem, using so much strength that he pulls off a long strip and the cloth gives way with a rip. Now, a loop. Favez is afraid. He must be quick. The crowd of rioters is roaring, still calling for his death... A very big loop. Favez stands up with the loop around his neck, ties one end to the bar in the door, and then launches himself forward. He hears his neck crack; at that moment there comes the sound of a key turning in the lock; it is the warder with his soup.

"What are you doing, Favez, for God's sake!"

The man has leapt on the prisoner; he pulls off the death-collar. Favez stands up, his glassy eyes quickly clearing; Favez rubs the nape of his neck, says nothing.

"So you wanted to die, Favez? You'd do better to keep your strength for the examinations and the trial. You'll need it. I heard your famous doctor just now in my lodge, he was talking with one of the judges; it won't be before winter."

Favez swallows his soup, his bread; nothing will disturb his lugubrious calm until the single visit paid him by his court-appointed lawyer. And the one the white lady would again be able to make at the end of July, in return for a generous bribe to the warder, as would also come out at the inquiry.

The visit by Favez's court-appointed lawyer, on Tuesday 21st July, in his cell in Oron:

"You are accused of violating three graves," Maître Maillard, of the firm of Maillard, Vinet and Veillard, 12 Rue de Bourg, Lausanne, states calmly. "In the cemeteries of Ropraz, Carrouge and Ferlens. Sexual acts and vampirization perpetrated on the corpses of three young women. Butchering and mutilation. In any case, disturbing the peace of the dead. Very serious crimes, Monsieur Favez! Of the three, Ropraz is the most serious – as you very well know, Monsieur Favez, Rosa was the judge's darling daughter... and purity itself, in the eyes of all. But no one can prove it was you who committed these three violations, of which you have been previously accused. So keep your mouth shut. At the hearing, remain silent. Given a fair trial, doubt will prevail and it will all work to your advantage."

Maître Maillard glances down at his notes, pauses for a moment, and then goes on:

"Two other charges are proven. At the Café du Nord, in Ferlens, a series of unnatural acts committed upon the cattle belonging to M. Georges Pasche. In Mézières, the rape of Mme Dubois, a widow. In both these cases the defence will be more difficult, because in the eyes of the court and in the minds of the jurors these facts clearly confirm the violations in the three cemeteries. Sexuality, bestiality, cruelty: let me remind you that several heifers belonging to M.

Pasche had their recta perforated with a sharp instrument, which does nothing to help our case. Do you follow me, M. Favez? And I must add one more thing: in a countryside where discontent and anger are rife, you are the ideal accused. A settling of accounts, the hatred of Judge Gilliéron, whose daughter was sacrificed... and you are the providential scapegoat, M. Favez. Unfortunately, there is the matter of those beasts. Perforated recta, a sharp instrument, bleeding membranes, a bad outcome – obviously the expected complement to the dismembering of the three dead young women..."

The lawyer breaks off again, as if bowed down by his task, and then looks Favez directly in the eye:

"For all these reasons, Favez, keep your mouth shut. Leave it to me to separate the graveyard incidents from the two other cases, which are, all the same, less extraordinary in a countryside hardly renowned for the purity of its morals. On the one hand the widow and the cows. On the other, your lechery-butchery..."

The lawyer is very pleased with his little word-play. He knows he will use it again in town; this brute of a client is incapable of appreciating it.

What Maître Maillard has not pointed out, because he has failed to appreciate the extent of the ferocious feelings of guilt oppressing this countryside, is that far from making Favez's cause more banal, the acts committed with the heifers and the rape of the widow Dubois weigh heavily on his case, for they are a reminder of too many shameful secrets in the villages round about. Foul things, dark and unspoken. Drink. Superstition. Incest. Ancient, furtive fornications in stables and cowsheds. Repeated cruelty to crazed animals. Meditated murders. Long-harboured vengeance.

Maître Maillard, this witty city lawyer, is too unfamiliar with the stifling, paralysing remorse concealed by the fresh landscape and sturdy physiques. He knows nothing of the dense derangement affecting minds and bodies. Of the evil beneath the idyll. Of the wish for death. Of the unspoken, skulking fear.

"Let me speak in court, Favez, I'll win those people over for you in a flash. I'm on your side, Favez. Stay confident. Say nothing. And I'll see you get out of this mess."

At that, the lawyer returns to his distinguished office on Rue de Bourg with his two partners and three secretaries, and the course he teaches in the Faculty of Law at the University of Lausanne.

# 14

Dr Mahaim has returned.

The mysterious white lady has returned.

After Dr Mahaim, a respite, a cunning, placid calm.

After the lady in white, tension, stupefaction, a terrible longing for love. An entire life, twenty-one years, a long, hard childhood, an adult too soon, the solitude of the body, always the wasteland of the heart. Like a confirmation, a sacred message that she gives him: "You made a mess of it, Charles-Augustin. Now you are Favez, a vampire for all eternity." This is the monster's ordination, just as for 2,000 years there has been an ordination of priests before the altar. *Sacerdos eris in aeternum. Vampyrus eris in aeternum.*

The lady comes closer, touches him, takes the Vampire's mouth in hers. "Did you play when you were little, Charles-Augustin? Were you weaned too soon? Animals that haven't suckled their mother don't know how to play. From the start they scratch to wound, bite to kill. You've never been a little child, Charles-Augustin. You were a child vampire. A child murderer. And I, I love you, Charles-Augustin."

The lady takes the Vampire's tongue in her mouth and gently nibbles it. The lady is trembling.

Is it this concentration of evil that attracts the white lady? The violence taut beneath this skin? Or the solitary man's fear? Or this smell of death, of earth full of death, of skin rubbed against death, of a member red with the blood of death? And all the victims are here, bound, cut open, trussed and devoured, within this lonely man who is trembling with desire and fear as he stands by the bed in his cell.

94

The lady takes into her mouth his member, stained with the blood of death. The lady sucks and swallows the Vampire in sharp little gulps.

The sepulchral lovemaking lasts an entire hour. An hour for which the lady pays twenty-five francs into the warder's greasy palm. Five shiny silver *écus* bearing the Federal mark. Enough to live less miserably for three months.

Will she come back again? No one knows. The warder will say no more. In certain beings there is a burning thirst for sacrifice and sexual crime. In many women. The white lady was one such. It is interesting how, in Favez's prison cell, she reconstructs, though in reverse, the abominable episode of the desecrated graves. In the graveyard it is the Vampire who cuts up and consumes his women victims; in the cell it is the woman who drinks the Vampire until he begs for mercy. A ritual in reverse that plunges Favez's history into strange, troubled emotions, while it makes you one of us, Vampire of Ropraz, my brother, my twin.

# 15

The trial goes badly for Favez. After five months of imprisonment the man is more sombre than ever and the anger has continued to grow, calling for his head or for life imprisonment. In the meantime several more incidents have been unearthed, forgotten cases have been reopened, and the trail picked up again of crimes it had been thought could safely be filed away. Girls with their clothes torn off after sunset, night-time assaults, unescorted women flung to the ground at a crossroads by someone impossible to identify, or swifter than an animal – again impossible to recognize him, but now it is known to be Favez. The Vampire Favez, Favez, always

Favez. In Ropraz, since he had no access to the young Jaunin child, despite numerous attempts to climb in and break down doors, a cow was bled in the Jaunin's meadow, its innards devoured on the spot. Already Favez. Favez again. At Corcelles one of the Porchet girls was followed along a hedgerow; she ran off and got away, but from afar she recognized Favez.

The presiding judge recalls her.

"What do you mean, recognized? How can you be sure? You were too far away to see him."

"He was laughing the way vampires do. Do you think I didn't see his teeth?"

The trial opened on 21st December, 1903, in Oron-la-Ville courthouse, with Charles Pasche as presiding judge.

Favez was represented by Maître Maillard.

The courtroom was packed. All eyes were on the very pale complexion, red-ringed eyes and long teeth of the accused.

"Enough to send shivers down your back," the first rows exclaim repeatedly.

The reading of the indictment arouses such fury

that the presiding judge threatens to break off this first session, and then to empty the courtroom.

From the outset, Favez makes a sorry impression, sniggering, remaining silent or, when pressed for an answer by the presiding judge, expressing himself in snatches and rumblings. "Nothing could be more like an animal", denounced the *Revue de Lausanne* in the unsparing account it gave. This is what it wrote in its issue for 22nd December:

We hope that the arguments will be presented decisively enough to allow an early decision. Since there can be no doubt about Favez's guilt, there is every reason to think that the case will be disposed of before the end of the year.

The tone was set. The court sat for four days. The dates and number of the sittings were as follows:

Monday the 21st of December: two sessions, morning and afternoon. Reading of the indictment, first hearing of evidence (six witnesses).

Tuesday the 22nd of December: two sessions, morning and afternoon. Remaining witnesses (eleven). Starting at two o'clock in the afternoon, Dr Mahaim's evidence.

Wednesday the 23rd of December: Closing speech for the prosecution. Maître Maillard for the defence. Consultation with the jury.

Thursday the 24th of December: judgement.

On the 24th of December at eleven-thirty in the morning, Charles-Augustin Favez, of Palézieux, born in Syens on the 2nd November, 1882, is condemned by the court of Oron-la-Ville to life imprisonment for all the acts of which he stands accused, none excepted, and with no attenuating circumstances. Given the extreme horror of the principal deeds committed by the said Favez, namely vampirism and the desecration of graves, the sentence includes twenty years in a high-security prison, without possibility of remittance.

The public stamps its feet in approval.

Dr Mahaim rushes to the rooms of President Pasche, out of sight of the crowd, and convinces the judge and jury, considering the obviously psychotic character of the crimes, which make them of scientific interest to the doctors and

100

students of the new establishment at Cery, to commute Favez's sentence to detention for life in the said psychiatric institution. The court therefore orders that the condemned man be conducted under heavy escort to a cell in the Cery clinic, in the municipality of Prilly, west of Lausanne, to be used for the study of mental illness by physicians and medical students of the canton.

On 24th December it is snowing and the cold is intense when Favez spends his first night at Cery, in his heavily padded cell.

On 25th December, two nurses in blue caps fetch him from his cell to take part in the Christmas festivities of the patients and staff. The candles are burning on the big tree, and Favez, the mental patients, nurses and doctors sing of Christ's birth, drink mulled wine and eat little cakes baked by volunteers in the kitchen.

# 16

Favez will spend twelve years in Cery. Three years confined to a cell, after which his good behaviour and athletic build allow him to be transferred to the hospital's model farm. There he works looking after the pigs, and later the cattle, for nine more years of his story.

In February 1915 Favez escapes, crosses the frontier by way of the Vallorbe forest, to arrive in a France at war, where he joins the French army as a foreign volunteer. Three weeks later he is posted to the Foreign Legion. Inquiries by the Swiss authorities have been able to establish that the volunteer first-class Charles-Augustin Favez joined the battalion of the Foreign Legion as an infantryman in the section led by the Swiss corporal Frédéric Sauser, the author of some poems under the pen name of Blaise Cendrars. This Cendrars welcomes him warmly, and, despite Favez's reticence, worms some confidences out of him for a book he intends to write one day on a mad eviscerator of young girls. He has even decided on the title already: *Moravagine*. A violator of young bodies, Favez, a violator of graves? No judgement is passed. The Legion and the War wipe slates clean.

Cendrars, Favez and their comrades are thrown into the breach on the northern front between the Marne and the Somme; they fight in the mud at Notre Dame de Lorette, at Vimy, at Bois de la Vache, always pushing northwards, towards Champagne-Pouilleuse. On 28th September, 1915, at 19.30 hrs, along the Souain road, about 200 yards from the Navarin farm, after several assaults that are violently repulsed, the unit of Corporal Sauser-Cendrars and Favez is again thrown into the attack on the German trench nicknamed the "Kultur". It is raining, it is muddy, and the Cendrars-Favez section comes under enemy fire. Blaise Cendrars' right forearm is shattered; he is carried to the rear and it is amputated. In the same fighting Favez is killed, his body left lying on the battlefield, every trace of him finally lost.

Until, that is, the Unknown Soldier is chosen by lot, on 21st November, 1920, from among eight coffins brought to the Fortress of Douaumont from all over the battle zones. The remains of a single anonymous hero above whom the eternal flame would burn beneath the glorious Arc de Triomphe.

For – and here we meet again – recent research has suggested that the remains of the Unknown Soldier, subjected to DNA analysis, belong to a native of the canton of Vaud, Charles-Augustin Favez, a volunteer enlisted in the French army at war in February 1915, and killed before the Navarin farm on 28th September of the same year. And that the Unknown Soldier – honoured as a hero by the Head of State, by the Last Post, and by the salute to the flag on every fourteenth of July – that God himself has made, may be none other than a deranged man and dreaded ex-convict of Swiss origin and dark memory in the hallucinatory annals of the living dead. Of course the ministries involved have suppressed the results of these analyses, and the scandal has been hushed up. So only a few of us suspect that under the glorious Arc de Triomphe, beneath the Unknown Soldier's eternal flame, lies Favez, the Vampire of Ropraz, sleeping lightly as he waits for other nights to be up and on the loose.